# Topsy and Tim
# Have Their Eyes Tested

**By Jean and Gareth Adamson**
**Consultant: Russell Peake BSc (hons) MCOptom, Boots Opticians**

LADYBIRD BOOKS

UK | USA | Canada | Ireland | Australia
India | New Zealand | South Africa

Ladybird Books is part of the Penguin Random House group of companies
whose addresses can be found at global.penguinrandomhouse.com
www.penguin.co.uk www.puffin.co.uk www.ladybird.co.uk

First published by Ladybird Books Ltd, 2017
001



www.topsyandtim.com

Printed in China

A CIP catalogue record for this book is available from the British Library

ISBN: 978–0–241–28254–0

All correspondence to:
Ladybird Books
Penguin Random House Children's
80 Strand, London WC2R 0RL

One morning, Mummy took Topsy and Tim to school.
They met Stevie Dunton and his mum on the way.
"Stevie is going to get his eyes checked at school today,"
said his mum.
"So are we," said Topsy and Tim.

At school, a special nurse tested the children's eyes. First, he checked how well the eyes worked together.

Topsy's eyes were covered and uncovered one at a time with a special tool called an occluder.
"You're doing very well to sit so still," said the nurse.

Next, the nurse held up cards with different pictures on. The children were asked to say what the pictures were from a long way off, one eye at a time.

Some of the pictures were very BIG. They were easy to see.
Some were quite small. They were more difficult.
Tim could see all the pictures easily.
Topsy could see them too, but she had to try harder.
Stevie couldn't see them very well at all.
He got them all wrong.

"Topsy had better go to the optician's," the nurse told Mummy.
He gave Mummy a letter for the optometrist.

After school, Tim and Mummy took Topsy to the optician's.
Stevie was there too, but he was in a grumpy mood.

Mrs Edmunds the optometrist took Topsy and Tim into her room. It was like a magic parlour. It had lots of interesting lights and gadgets.

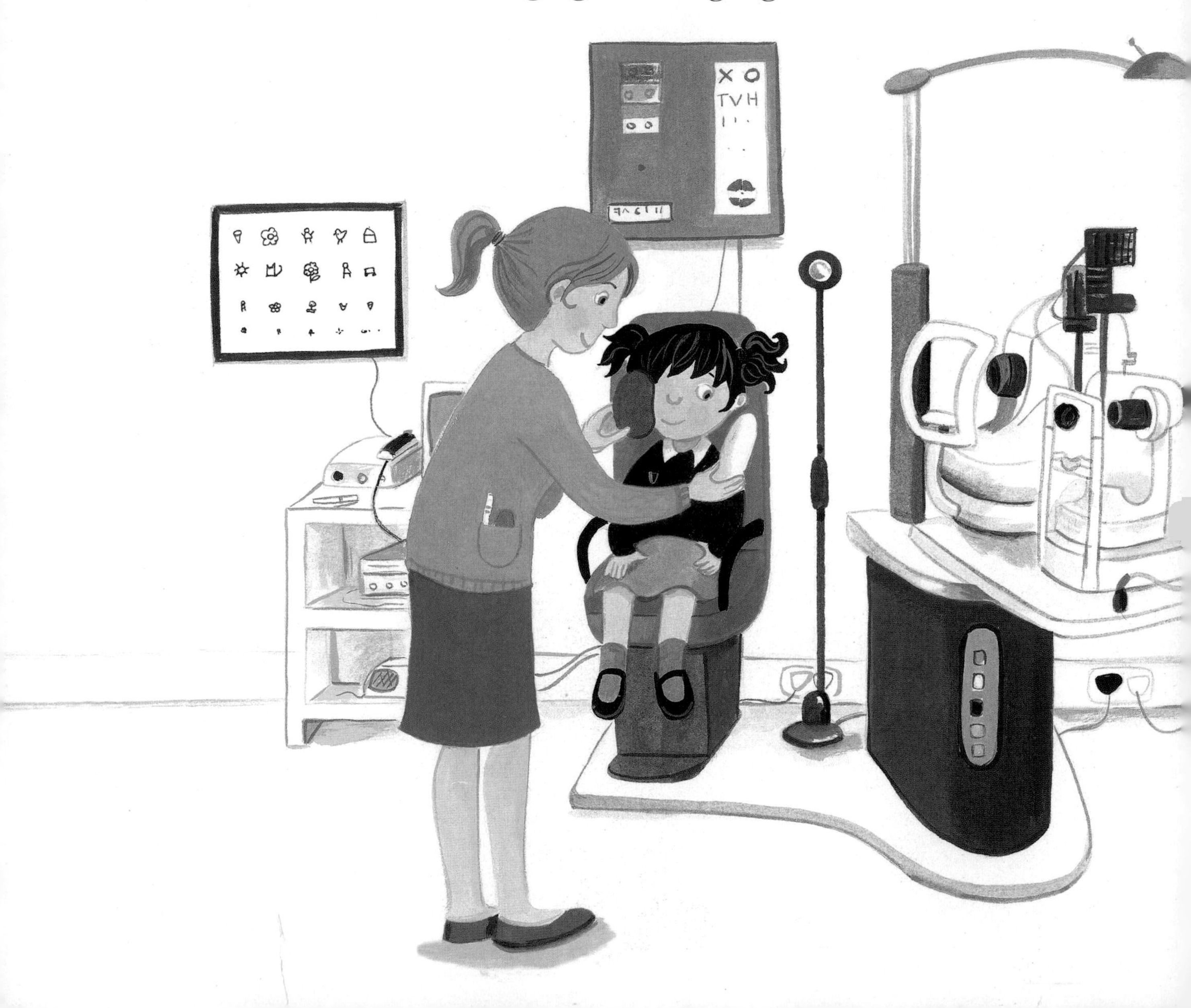

Mrs Edmunds tested each of Topsy's eyes in turn. "I would like Topsy to come back for more tests another day," she said to Mummy.

Stevie had his eyes tested next. Mrs Edmunds found that Stevie was short-sighted, which meant he found it difficult to see things far away. She put some special frames on Stevie and slipped some glass lenses into them. Stevie looked like a spaceman, but he could see clearly now.

"We will have a nice pair of glasses made,
just for you," said Mrs Edmunds.
"Don't want glasses," said Stevie, grumpily.

Mrs Edmunds measured Stevie so that his glasses would fit properly.

Mrs Edmunds' assistant helped Stevie choose frames for his glasses.

"They will be ready for you in a few days' time," he said. "Won't that be nice?"

"No," said Stevie.

A few days later, Topsy went back for more tests.
Mrs Edmunds put some special drops in Topsy's eyes.
"Do they hurt?" asked Tim.
"No, they just feel funny," said Topsy. "A little bit tingly."

Topsy and Tim and Mummy went for a walk, to give the eye drops time to work. The black middles of Topsy's blue eyes grew big. That meant it was time to go back to Mrs Edmunds.

"Now your pupils are nice and big I will be able to look into them easily and check if you need glasses," said Mrs Edmunds. She turned the room lights out and looked into Topsy's eyes with her own special little light.

"Topsy's eyes are quite all right," Mrs Edmunds told Mummy. "She doesn't need glasses."

On their way out, they met Stevie again.
He had come to get his new glasses.
Topsy and Tim liked Stevie's new glasses –
but Stevie didn't.

Early the next morning, Stevie's mum came
to see Topsy and Tim.

"Please will you walk to school with Stevie today?" she asked them. "He has got his new glasses on, and he is feeling shy."

Stevie's new glasses made him look clever.
Topsy told him so.

Stevie was not grumpy any more.
"I can see better than Topsy and Tim now," he laughed.
"You must be wearing SUPERSPECS!" said Tim.

*Now turn the page and help*
*Topsy and Tim solve a puzzle.*

Topsy and Tim are having their eyes tested.
Look at the different picture cards and see
if you can find the matching pairs.

Once you've found the pairs, why not colour them in?

A Map of the Village
farm
Topsy and Tim's house
Tony's house
Kerr
hou
park

garage
post office
health centre
church
primary school
nursery school
police station

# Have you read all the Topsy and Tim stories?

☐ 9781409300564

☐ 9781409300618

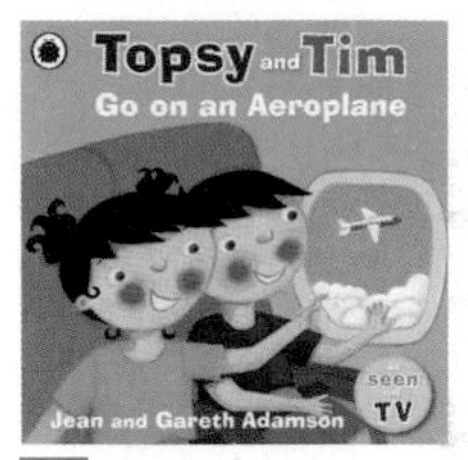


☐ 9781409300571

☐ 9781409303350

☐ 9781409304241

☐ 9781409300601

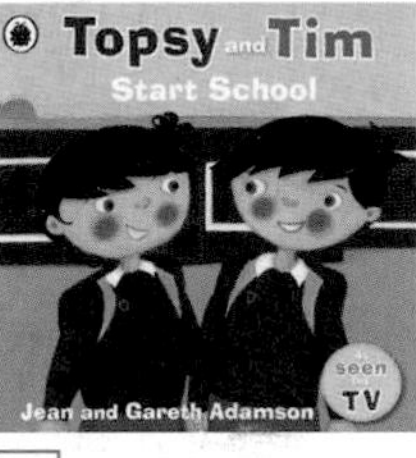


☐ 9781409300830

☐ 9781409303336

☐ 9781409304234

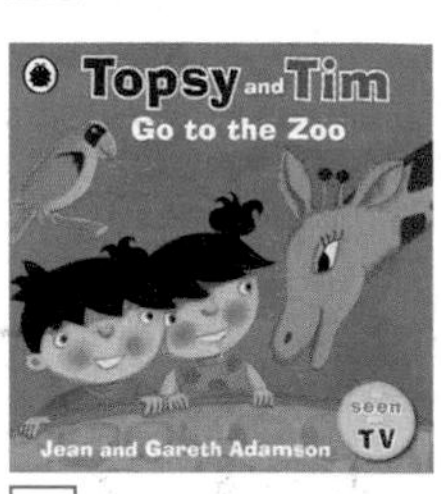


☐ 9781409300847

☐ 9781409300588

☐ 9781409303367

☐ 9781409303343

☐ 9781409307204

☐ 9781409307211

☐ 9781409308829

☐ 9781409308836

☐ 9781409309468

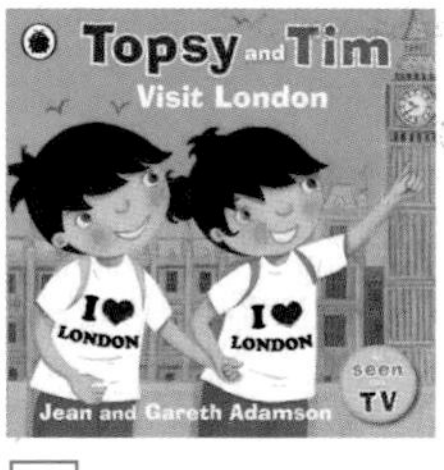


☐ 9781409309475

☐ 9781409311591

☐ 9780723292593

☐ 9780723292586

☐ 9780241189702

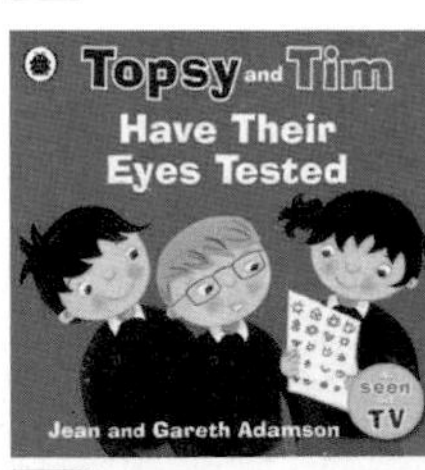


☑ 9780241282540

**This Topsy and Tim book belongs to**

______________________